Fife Council Education Department
King's Road Primary School
King's Crescent, Rosyth KY11 2RS

Let's
Explore

Changing seasons

by Henry Pluckrose

W
FRANKLIN WATTS
NEW YORK • LONDON • SYDNEY

Author's note

This book is one of a series which has been designed to encourage young readers to think about the everyday concepts that form part of their world. The text and photographs complement each other, and both elements combine to provide starting points for discussion. Although each book is complete in itself, each title links closely with others in the set, so presenting an ideal platform for learning.

I have consciously avoided 'writing down' to my readers. Young children like to know the 'real' words for things, and are better able to express themselves when they can use correct terms with confidence.

Young children learn from the experiences they share with adults around them. The child offers his or her ideas which are then developed and extended through the adult. The books in this series are a means for the child and adult to share informal talk, photographs and text, and the ideas which accompany them.

One particular element merits comment. Information books are also reading books. Like a successful story book, an effective information book will be turned to again and again. As children develop, their appreciation of the significance of fact develops too. The young child who asks 'Why do we need clocks?' may subsequently and more provocatively ask, 'Who invented time?' Thoughts take time to generate. Hopefully books like those in this series provide the momentum for this.

Henry Pluckrose

Contents

Short, cold days and
long, dark nights.
Rain, wind, frost and snow.
Cold fingers and toes.
It's the season of winter.

In winter the sun
is low in the sky.
The weather is cold
and the trees have no leaves.

When the weather is cold,
we wear thick clothes which
keep us cosy and warm.

Some animals grow
thick coats for the winter.
Others find a place
to curl up and sleep
until the weather is warmer.
This is called hibernation.

Winter slowly turns to spring.

The sun begins to warm the earth.

Trees and plants
start to bud and flower.

Many animals wake up
from their winter sleep.
Birds make nests
and lay their eggs.

Spring turns to summer.
The sun is hot, so we wear
thin clothes which keep us cool.
Summer is the warmest
season of the year.

In summer we can spend
lots of time outdoors.
It is a good season
for holidays, for picnics
and enjoying the sunshine.

Hot summer weather sometimes brings storms. Rain can make the air feel fresh and cool again.

As summer turns to autumn, farmers harvest their crops.

Some animals are harvesting, too.
This squirrel is collecting nuts
to make a store of food
to last the winter months.

In autumn, the colder weather turns the leaves of the trees to shades of red, yellow and orange.

In autumn, many birds
fly to warmer countries
to spend the winter there.
This is called migration.

Winter, spring, summer, autumn. A whole year has passed and winter is here again!

Index

First published in 2000 by
Franklin Watts
96 Leonard Street
London
EC2A 4XD

Franklin Watts Australia
14 Mars Road
Lane Cove
NSW 2066

Copyright © Franklin Watts 2000

ISBN 0 7496 3660 2

Dewey Decimal
Classification Number 574.5

A CIP catalogue record for this book is
available from the British Library

Series editor: Louise John
Series designer: Jason Anscomb

Printed in Hong Kong

Picture Credits:
Steve Shott Photography, cover page, pp. 25,
26; Ray Moller Photography, title page, pp. 8,
9, 17; Robert Harding p. 6 (Cathy Collins) 27
(Jacobs), 31 (Robert Estall); Oxford Scientific
Films p. 10 (Owen Newman); Eye
Ubiquitous p. 12 (P. Claydon), 16, 19 (Yiorgos
Nikiteas); Bruce Coleman
p. 14/15 (Dr Eckart Pott), 23 (Andrew
Purcell), 24 (Jane Burton), 28 (Bruce
Coleman); Image Bank p. 20 (Pete Turner);
Tony Stone Images p. 4 (Lori Adamski Peek).
With thanks to: Victoria Harris